To: Ryan Johnson

Merry Christmas 2016

From: Lunnasting Primary School

A Fright
in the
Night

Written by Russell Punter

Illustrated by Gerald Guerlais

How this book works

The story of **A Fright in the Night** has been written for you to read with your child. You take turns to read:

You read these words.

> The house is dark,
> the blinds are drawn.

> "I'm Jess the vet.
> You must be Bill?"

> But wait –
> is that a light?

> Yes, Jess,
> that is right.

Your child reads these words.

You don't have to finish the story in one session. If your child is getting tired, put a marker in the page and come back to it later.

You can find out more about helping your child with this book, and with reading in general, on pages 30-31.

A Fright
in the
Night

Turn the page to start the story.

The house is dark,
the blinds are drawn.

But wait –
is that a light?

"I have some pets
that need your help.
This way please,
follow me."

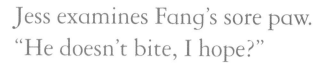
Jess examines Fang's sore paw.
"He doesn't bite, I hope?"

9

"And now please check my fish,"
    says Bill.
"I think they must be sick."

Jess checks the pair all over,
to find out why they're ill.

Yes, yes, I see.
It's not too bad.

17

Jess soon spots the problem.
She finds a tooth that's split.

"Bill, look at that.
This tooth is bad."

When Jess has done,
Bill shows her out.

Jess looks at Bill,
and sees his... *teeth*!

Puzzle 1

Match the sentences to the pictures
on the opposite page.

1. He can see the sun.

2. His foot is red.

3. She has to run!

4 His tooth is bad.

A

B

C

D

Puzzle 2

Look at the pictures, then choose
the right sentence.

1.

A "I will reed to soak his foot."

B "I will need to soak his foot."

2.

A "A pill will fix them, Bill."

B "A pill will mix them, Bill."

3.

A "Is he in a good moon?"

B "Is he in a good mood?"

4.

A "So long, I need to run!"

B "So song, I need to run!"

Puzzle 3

Find the words that rhyme. The first pair has already been linked as an example.

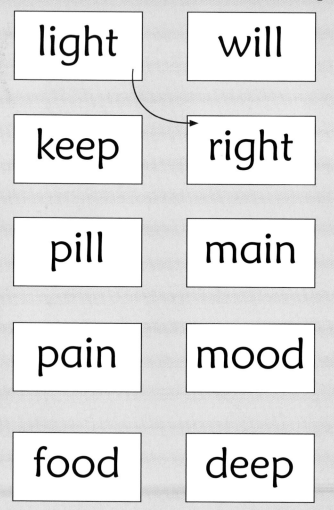

light	will
keep	right
pill	main
pain	mood
food	deep

Answers to puzzles

Puzzle 1

1. He can see the sun. – C

2. His foot is red. – A

3. She has to run! – D

4. His tooth is bad. – B

Puzzle 2

1. B "I will need to soak his foot."

2. A "A pill will fix them, Bill."

3. B "Is he in a good mood?"

4. A "So long, I need to run!"

Puzzle 3

light ~~~ right

keep ~~~ deep

pill ~~~ will

pain ~~~ main

food ~~~ mood

Guidance notes

Usborne Very First Reading is a series of books, specially developed for children who are learning to read. In the early books in the series, you and your child take turns to read, and your child steadily builds the knowledge and confidence to read alone.

The words for your child to read in **A Fright in the Night** introduce these letter-combinations:

(Note that in standard English, **oo** can be pronounced either as in 'look' or as in 'moon' – both are used in this story.) It's well worth giving your child plenty of practice reading these. Later books in the series gradually introduce more letter-combinations and spelling patterns, while reinforcing the ones your child already knows.

You'll find lots more information about the structure of the series, advice on helping your child with reading, extra practice activities and games on the Very First Reading website,* www.usborne.com/veryfirstreading

*US readers go to www.veryfirstreading.com

Some questions and answers

- **Why do I need to read with my child?**
  Sharing stories and taking turns makes reading an enjoyable and fun activity for children. It also helps them to develop confidence and reading stamina, and to take part in an exciting story using very few words.

- **When is a good time to read?**
  Choose a time when you are both relaxed, but not too tired, and there are no distractions. Only read for as long as your child wants to — you can always try again another day.

- **What if my child gets stuck?**
  Don't simply read the problem word yourself, but prompt your child and try to find the right answer together. Similarly, if your child makes a mistake, go back and look at the word together. Don't forget to give plenty of praise and encouragement.

- **We've finished, now what do we do?**
  It's a good idea to read the story several times to give your child more practice and confidence. Then you can try reading **The Queen Makes a Scene** at the same level or, when your child is ready, go on to Book 7 in the series.

Edited by Jenny Tyler, Lesley Sims
and Mairi MacKinnon

First published in 2011 by Usborne Publishing Ltd., Usborne House,
83-85 Saffron Hill, London EC1N 8RT, England. www.usborne.com
Copyright © 2011 Usborne Publishing Ltd.

USBORNE VERY FIRST READING

There are over thirty titles in the **Usborne Very First Reading** series, which has been specially developed to help children learn to read. Here are some of them.

To find out more about the structure of the series, go to
www.usborne.com/veryfirstreading

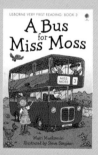

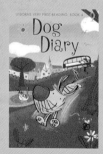